THE FRANK SHOW

David Mackintosh

HarperCollins *Children's Books*

First published in hardback in Great Britain by
HarperCollins Children's Books in 2012

10 9 8 7 6 5 4 3 2 1

ISBN 978-0-00-736400-8

HarperCollins Children's Books is a division of HarperCollins Publishers Ltd.

Text and illustrations copyright © David Mackintosh 2012

Designed and lettered by David Mackintosh
www.davidmackintosh.co.uk

Visit our website at: www.harpercollins.co.uk

Printed and bound by Printing Express, Hong Kong

My grandad's name is Frank.

Frank lives at our house and he's always around.

Frank talks about what things were like when he was a boy my age. He says, "Things were a lot tougher back then."

Frank says that it was a lot quieter when he was my age. *"You could hear yourself think!"* he yells.

My teacher has asked us to talk about one member of our family for show and tell on Friday. We can choose one person and talk for one minute, about the things they like and what kind of person they are.

I ask Mum if I can talk about her but she says that
she is very busy and that I should speak to my father
when he gets off the phone.

Dad says why don't I talk about Minnie, my sister?
Minnie won't make a good subject to talk about,
so I tell him I'll think about it.

The only person left is Frank.
But Frank is just a grandad.

Frank always says,

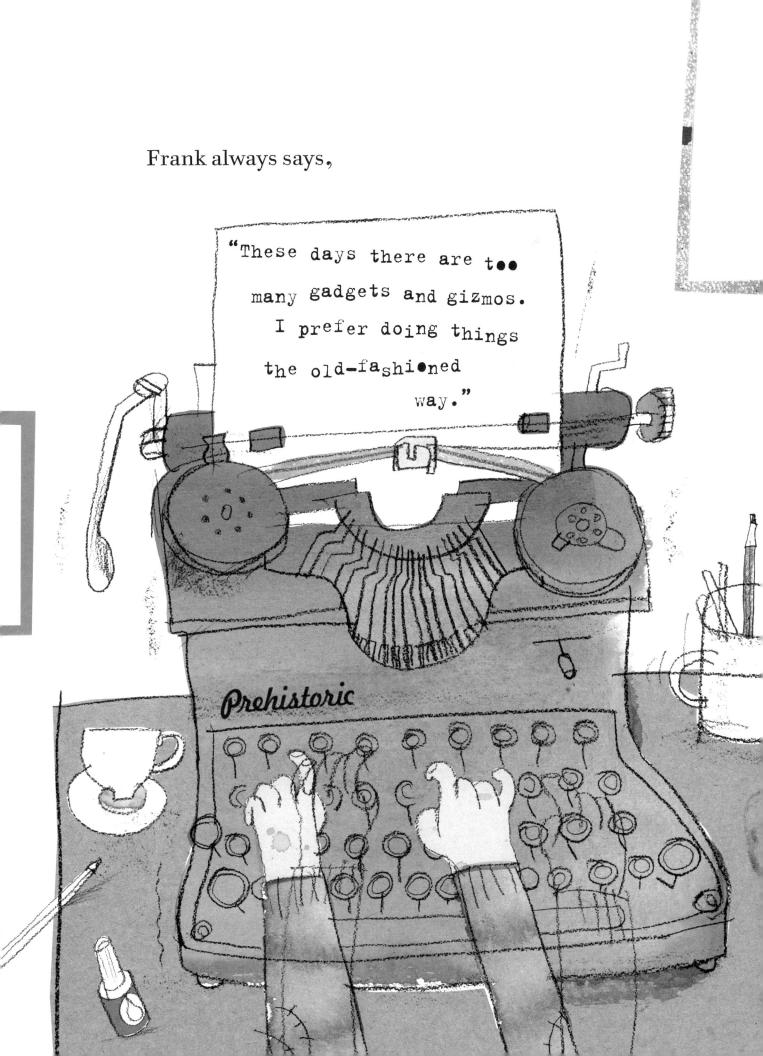

"These days there are too many gadgets and gizmos. I prefer doing things the old-fashioned way."

Today I told my teacher that Mum was very busy and Dad had had a very long day, so the only person left in my family to talk about was Frank, my grandad.
She said, "*Fabulous!*", but I don't know about that.

At home, Frank says he doesn't like 'fancy' food.
"Plain and simple, that's me," he reckons.

I wonder if there is *anything* about Frank that will make my talk interesting.

On Tuesday at the shops, Frank says he only needs his hair cut once a year and he doesn't trust barbers. He says, "If it ain't broke, don't fix it. I can do without their input."

And I just have mine tidied up.

My friend Tom says that his Uncle Marlon is a musician who plays drums on the radio. Tom says he's allowed to bring his drumsticks on Friday. *His uncle is cool.*

That night, I ask Frank if he can play a musical instrument. Maybe an electrical guitar?

Frank says, "Today's music is just noise and you can't understand the words."

He only likes
listening to
his music
and says,

"**They
don't
make
'em
like
that
any more.**"

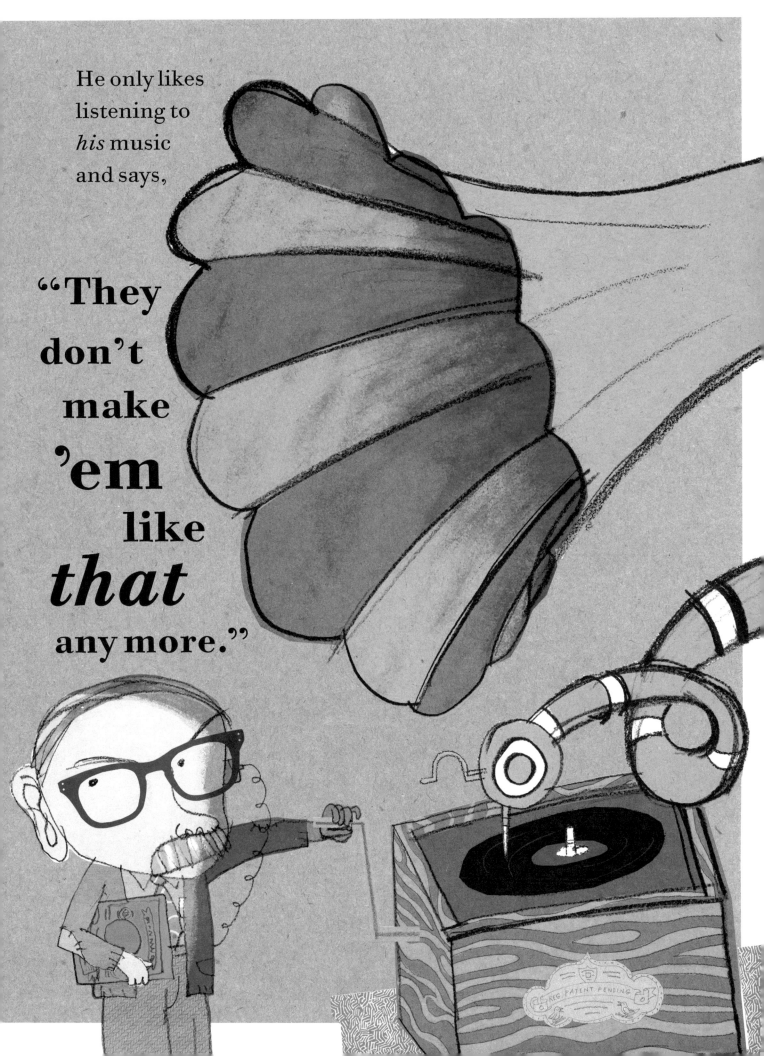

Barbara Bailey told me that she's going to bring
a colour photo of her nan's mobility scooter.
Her nan's a retiree and secretary of a bowls club.

Maybe I should take a
colour photo of Frank?

That night, I ask Frank why
he doesn't drive a scooter
or play bowls.

Frank says, "Doctors speak a lot of mumbo-jumbo
and bowls is dull as old dishwater."

He doesn't trust doctors as far as he can throw them,
which isn't far on account of his arm.
And one of his hips.

Kristian's dad is a comedian on TV who makes everyone laugh. Paolo's mum is Italian and knows all about Italian and can speak Italian. Fay's cousin tells you if your bag's too heavy at the airport. Donny's dad works in a crisp factory. Saul's aunt swam the English Channel. Hugo's stepbrother has a sports car, with an eightball gear knob.

My grandad's arm
hurts when it's
about to rain.

I wish I could choose Tom. He's my age and I've known him since January. Tom carries a full deck of Modern Marvels Flash Cards in his back pocket and I'm the only other person he lets hold them. He's smaller than me, but that doesn't matter when you're best friends.

Tom asked me why I chose Frank for my talk, because Frank's just a grandad.

I didn't know what to say.

So now Tom and me aren't speaking.

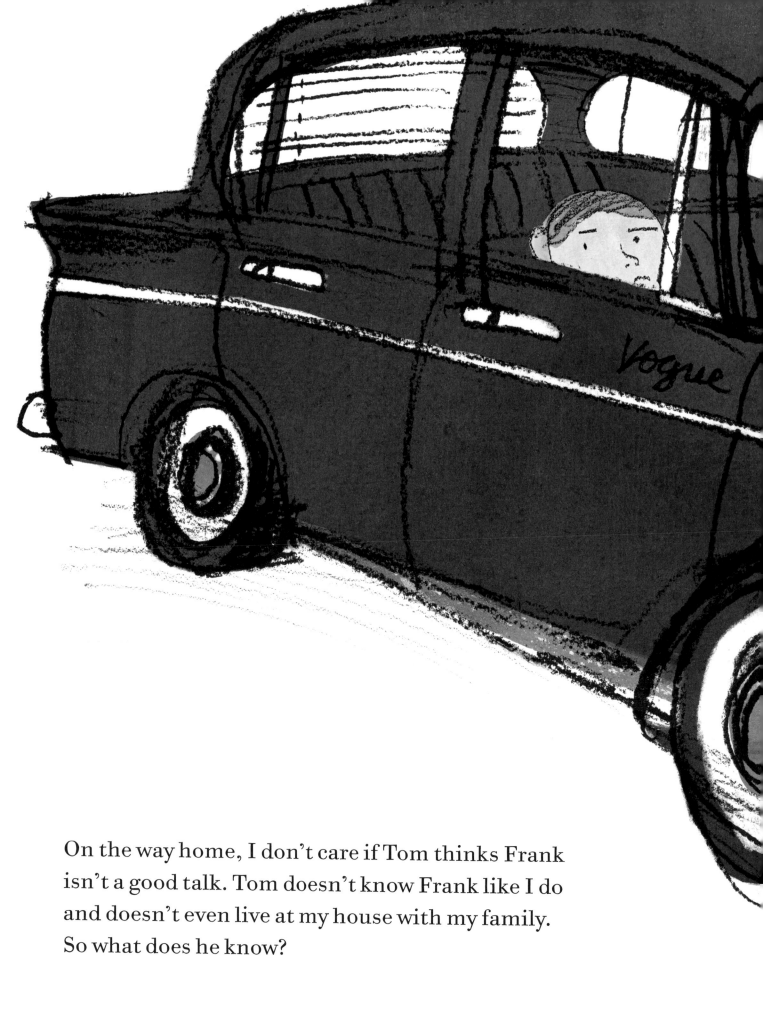

On the way home, I don't care if Tom thinks Frank isn't a good talk. Tom doesn't know Frank like I do and doesn't even live at my house with my family. So what does he know?

But then, Tom might be right, because everyone has someone interesting to talk about. And Frank is, well... just my grandad.

My grandad doesn't always like the way things are.
And he always does things his way.

He doesn't like noise, **or** today's music, **or** gadgets and gizmos (**or** new things), **or** haircuts, **or** weather, **or** doctors, **or** any sort of ice cream that isn't vanilla. **And** today I have to talk all about him for a *full minute*.

In class, everyone is excited.
They have all spoken for a full minute each about a
member of their family, even Clive Martin. Then we all
have to look out of the window to see Hannah's mum's
company car.

Everyone in my class has someone
interesting to show and tell.

But now it's my turn to talk about...

Frank.

I tell them everything I know about Frank...

how Frank doesn't like noise, **or** today's music,
or gadgets and gizmos (**or** new things), **or** haircuts,
or weather, **or** doctors, **or** anything but vanilla,
and about how everything was a lot tougher when
he was a boy my age.

And... *that's it.*

I've run out of things I can say about Frank,
and everyone is looking straight at me,

when...

Frank begins to tell a story about how he led an army in a charge across a muddy battlefield…

with bullets whistling all around like African bees…

and how the whole way he didn't miss a single note on his bugle…

except when an explosion made him play a sharp instead of a flat…

and how he gave his last drop of water to a thirsty horse…

and captured one hundred enemy soldiers with nothing but his wit and brute force…

and how later… he and his buddies had a green tattoo put on their arms to remember that day.

Frank explains how he has a piece of metal
left in his elbow from when he was in the war.
"And every time it's about to rain,
I know because my arm goes numb."

Sheldon Robe asks if getting a blurry
tattoo hurts and Frank winks and says,
"You bet it did, *hombre*."

Then we all have lunch.

He is olde
than all o
our birthda
added up.

And everybody cheered for my grandad Frank and me.

On the way home, Tom asked if he could
visit Frank and me at our house one day
and I said, "You bet you can, *hombre*."